Contents

1

A Scream

Somewhere in the darkness,
Greg heard a scream.
Night was closing in across the swamp.
The air was warm and heavy
now the wet season had begun.
It was a sticky night to be camping
out in the bush.

Greg stopped and looked up.
He was about to light the camp stove.
He peered out into the gloom.
The sky was almost dark.
Where did that scream come from?
Or maybe it was just a dingo
calling to its mate.
There were many noises of the night
in this part of Australia.

The drumming of rain on the camper van
was the only sound once more.
Perhaps it wasn't a scream after all.
Greg was about to strike a match to light the
gas when he heard it again.
Far away.
It was somewhere beyond the water.
Somewhere in the middle of the swamp.

Now he knew without doubt –
it was a girl's scream.

Swamp

Attack

John Townsend

Published in association with
The Basic Skills Agency

Hodder & Stoughton

A MEMBER OF THE HODDER HEADLINE GROUP

Acknowledgements
Cover: Darren Hopes
Illustrations: Chris Coady

Orders: please contact Bookpoint Ltd, 130 Milton Park, Abingdon, Oxon OX14
4SB. Telephone: (44) 01235 827720, Fax: (44) 01235 400454. Lines are open from
9.00–6.00, Monday to Saturday, with a 24 hour message answering service. You
can also order through our website: www.hodderheadline.co.uk.

British Library Cataloguing in Publication Data
A catalogue record for this title is available from The British Library

ISBN 0 340 87670 0

First published 2003
This edition published 2002
Impression number   10 9 8 7 6 5 4 3 2 1
Year   2007 2006 2005 2004 2003

Typeset by SX Composing DTP, Rayleigh, Essex.
Printed in Great Britain for Hodder & Stoughton Educational, a division of
Hodder Headline, 338 Euston Road, London NW1 3BH by Athenaeum Press
Ltd., Gateshead, Tyne and Wear.

2
A Dreadful Night

'Did you hear that?'
Greg called to the other campers.
A few vans were parked in a line.
He didn't know all the people at the camp.
'Hey! Did anyone hear that?'
No one said a word.
They were all too busy to notice.

Greg looked up and down the line of vans.
They all had lights on.
The campers were cooking or eating.
All but one van.
It was in darkness.
No one was there.
That was odd.

Val should have been back by now.
It was far too late for her to be out there alone.
She was nowhere to be seen.
Nor was the canoe she'd hired for the day.
This was no night to be out there.
The rain was now teeming down.
By morning the whole area
would be under water.

Greg jumped on to his quad bike.
Its engine roared
as he sped off in a spray of mud.
He headed down to the edge of the swamp.
The bike couldn't go any further
in the deep slush.
Greg looked across the miles
of empty water and scrub.
It was all so still.

'Hello! Can you hear me?'
Nothing.
No one could survive for long out there alone.
Greg turned the bike and sped back to camp.
He'd get the other rangers.
He'd get the boat.
He feared the worst.

Time and the rising water
were already against them.
He didn't tell anyone else
but he had other fears.
There were wild creatures out there.
Hungry.

3
Being Watched

Val had got up early that morning.
She was staying for a few days on her own,
in a camper van at East Alligator River.
It was good walking country.
There were no towns for hundreds of miles.
Val loved hiking in the great outdoors.
This was the place to be!

Val wanted to get a close look at the wildlife.
She wanted to get close to the rivers
to see the masses of birds.
That was why she hired the canoe.
It would be easy to paddle up streams
and across pools to look at nests.

Later on, thunder clouds began to bubble up.
Thin drizzle fell and the sky turned quite dark.
Suddenly Val felt uneasy.
Somehow she felt someone was watching her.
She looked round.
Nothing moved in the shadows.
Silence.
She was scared.

Val stopped to eat.
She had to empty the canoe of all the rain.
But this place had a nasty feel to it.
Val wanted to get back to camp.
She just didn't like it here.
She wanted to feel safe.
She turned the canoe round . . .
but it meant going back through the place
where she'd felt the eyes watch her.

She saw a lump of wood in the water.
It was floating near to her canoe.
She didn't take much notice . . .
until she saw the eyes.
They were bright yellow
and staring right at her.

4
Attack

The lump of wood was not a log at all.
A large crocodile swam towards the canoe.
A chill of fear shot up Val's spine.
'Keep calm,' she told herself.
'Crocs don't harm boats.'
She said it over and over again.
'Crocs don't harm boats.'

The crocodile's tail swept through the water.
This was a large saltie
(a man-eating salt water crocodile).
'If I keep away from him,
he'll just watch me float past,'
she told herself.

She lifted a paddle slowly.
But the current was faster here.
The canoe was swept along.
However much Val pushed on the paddle,
the canoe went its own way.
It was heading right for those staring eyes.
Towards the waiting jaws.
There was nothing she could do.
With a sudden bang and a spray,
the canoe spun as the crocodile struck.

Val froze in terror.
Her canoe rocked from side to side.
She clung on for life
as her flimsy boat rose from the water.
'No, please! I don't mean any harm!'
But the huge reptile wouldn't give up.
Its head and tail cracked against the hull.
It was huge.
This croc could be five metres long.

Val had to think fast.
She looked to her right.
There was a sand bank she could aim for.
But even if she got there,
she would have to wade through the water.
A croc this size could run
faster than any human.
There was nowhere to hide.

On her left, Val saw the steep muddy bank.
It was like a cliff just over two metres high.
A few small trees grew from it.
The lower branches hung over the water.
She might be able to grab hold of a branch
and pull herself up.
If she got up into a tree,
the croc would soon give up and swim away.
It was her only hope.

The tree trunks shone with wet and slimy moss.
She would try to grab hold of a branch.
It was the only way she could get out of the
water where the croc was now thrashing
in a rage.

Val pushed with her paddle
as hard as she could.
She fought against the current.
Slowly the bank came closer.
The angry yellow eyes never blinked.
Their evil stare was fixed on Val's terrified face.
She could only push on
and pray like never before.
The jaws opened in an evil grin . . .
ready to snap.

5

Holding on to Life

Val tried to stand up.
The canoe rocked under her.
'Go away. Leave me alone. Please!'
She couldn't hide her fear.
And the crocodile knew she was scared.

The front of the canoe touched the bank.
Rows of teeth waited for her to fall.
The trees came within reach.
If she could grab the first branch,
she could pull herself clear of the canoe.
She would have to be fast.
She jumped and swung from the branch.

In a flash, the croc shot from the water.
It leapt over the canoe with a roar.
Val didn't stand a chance.
Mid-air, the jaws snapped with a crack.
They smashed shut around Val's legs.
Teeth ripped into Val's shorts.
The croc tore her from the tree
and threw her down into the river.

She felt no pain at first.
The croc pulled her to the river bed.
It turned over and over.
This was the dreaded death roll.
The muddy water was black.
It filled her lungs.
She couldn't breathe.
It twisted her over and over
then shook her like a rag doll.

Suddenly all went still.
The croc kept hold of her legs.
It clamped her in its jaws
while it waited for her to drown.

Her chest was ready to burst.
Her mouth was full of slime.
She opened her eyes.
Her head was just below the surface.
Maybe she could lift her mouth
just high enough.
Val pushed her mouth above the water.
Air rushed into her lungs.
Her body filled with life once more.

She sucked in as deep and hard as she could.
Maybe she could pull herself free.
Anything was worth a try.
Just above her she saw a tree root on the bank.
It was just out of reach.
She gave a quick kick.
The croc lost its hold.
It opened its jaws to get a better grip.

That gave her the chance she needed.
She threw herself towards the root.
She pulled herself from the water.
Blood ran down her legs. Her feet slipped.
Her hands slid on the wet bark.
Once again the croc sprang from the river.

6

All Hope is Lost

The huge jaws tore into the top of Val's leg.
She screamed.
The pain ripped through her body.
With one quick shake of its head,
the croc tore Val from the tree once more.
They fell back in the river.
She'd now lost all hope.

Teeth dug into Val's thigh.
The end couldn't be long now.
She thought of her family.
She thought of her friends.
They'd never know what happened to her.
She could only give a cry
as the croc began to roll her again.

She reached down to the animal's mouth.
Her fingers touched its snout.
They found two sockets.
If she jabbed its eyes it might let go.
But it might go really mad.
She took the risk and dug in her nails.
Nothing happened.
It was its nose instead of its eyes.

Again and again she was whipped round.
Once or twice her head came up
to let her gasp in some air.
Once again she got a chance to grab a branch.
She held on for all she was worth.
Once again the croc seemed to rest.

For a split second it let go.
It needed to grab her higher up her body.
It waited before the final lunge.
That gave Val her chance.
This time she couldn't make a mistake.
With super human strength,
she pulled herself to the tree trunk.

A cliff of mud and rocks stretched above her.
The croc thrashed towards her.
Its throat growled,
its eyes flashed
and its jaws were ready . . .

7

'I've done it!'

Val flung herself up the bank.
But the mud was too slippery.
She slipped back.
Once more she dug her fingers into the mud
to pull herself up.
The top of the bank seemed to slip out of reach.
The croc was just behind her.
Her nails dug into the soft bank.
In a final burst of fear, she clung to the top.
She couldn't believe her luck.
Without looking back,
she fell down the other side.

As she crawled over mud and grass,
Val felt a surge of joy.
She was alive!
But she had to keep going.
With every step she was safer.
She stumbled on.
Step after painful step.

At last she fell in a heap.
She lay gasping for breath.
She looked up into the rain . . .
and she began to laugh!
'I've done it! I've got away!'
It was only then, as the silence came back,
that Val felt pain.

Her legs were in a mess.
She just knew she had to get help.
But how could she?
She was miles from camp.
The swamp was all around her.
Streams and rivers cut across miles of mud.
And the water was rising.
Other crocs could be waiting.

The bleeding wouldn't stop.
A bit of her thigh was hanging loose.
Her knees were ripped.
She tried to get to her feet.
Her muscle was torn.
It was agony to walk.
But she had to go on.
She had to get away.
She just had to find help . . .
before night began to fall.

8

One Last Scream

The rain poured down.
The warm swamps grew dark.
Steam rose from the lakes.
Val grew colder.
She felt dizzy but she had to keep going.
On and on towards camp.

Maybe she was doomed after all.
Had she gone through all that fear
only to die lost in a bog?
It all seemed so cruel.
If she fainted, that would be the end.
She could drown or die from loss of blood.
No one would ever know the truth.

Darkness was closing in.
She needed to rest.
How she wanted to sleep.
But she had to fight and keep going.
Step after step.
Stream after stream.
Mile after mile.

Like the light, all hope began to fade.
There was no way Val would
ever make it back to camp.
She knew that now.
Even if they sent a search party,
they'd never find her.
She would never survive the night.

Val couldn't go much further.
She was weak and dizzy.
Her leg was in a bad way.
Tears ran down her cheeks.
She yelled at the top of her voice,
'Val, you can do it. You know you can.
You MUST! Never give up.'

She knew the camp was somewhere
beyond the sheet of flood water.
But she would never get across now.
She lay down in the wet mud.
A dingo howled behind some trees.
Pulling herself to her knees,
she let out a scream.
'Help! Someone help me!'

She lay in a puddle.
The air was still.
Rain fell around her.
As she looked up at the dark sky,
Val took a deep breath.
Before she sank into sleep,
she gave one last scream.
There was no more she could do now.

9
A Miracle

Greg was sure he heard a cry.
He looked out across the black water.
Someone needed help out there.
He spun the bike round
and raced back to raise the alarm.

Val lay in a daze as the flies began to bite her.
She drifted in and out of sleep.
Suddenly she heard a motor.
'Help!' She tried to yell
but her voice was weak.
'I'm over here. Help!'

The boat came closer.
Greg heard a call above the roar of the motor.
'Keep shouting,' he called.
'We'll find you. But keep calling!'
She did. She yelled with every breath.
At last, the boat chugged along beside her.
Greg jumped out and held her.
He lifted her into the boat.
It was five hours since the attack.

It took many more hours to rush her to hospital.
Darwin was over 100 miles away.
Greg was amazed at how brave Val had been.
So were the doctors.
Her story hit the news.
Val was ill for a long time.
She had been badly hurt.
Germs got into her blood.
She had to stay over a month in one hospital.
Then she spent another month
having skin grafts.
At one time they said Val
would never walk again.
But she did. She proved them wrong.
Some said it was nothing less than a miracle.
....

This is a true story.
That makes it even more of a *chiller*.
But Val lived to tell the tale.
Perhaps she was just lucky.
Perhaps she was very brave.
But she never gave up.
She refused to give in.
Her state of mind saved her life.

Val even felt sorry for the crocodile!
She begged Greg not to shoot it.
After all, it was her mistake.
She was the one who was 'out of bounds'.
She never blamed the croc,
as it wasn't his fault.
Even today, she still says 'Sorry, crocodile!'
After all, it's not often
a tasty snack fights back!